W9-BGA-830

WALT DISNEY'S CLASSIC

Lady and the TRAMP

Based on Walt Disney's
full-length animated classic.

Adapted by Jan Carr.

SCHOLASTIC INC.
New York Toronto London Auckland Sydney

Scholastic Books are available at special discounts for quantity purchases for use as premiums, promotional items, retail sales through specialty market outlets, etc. For details contact: Special Sales Manager, Scholastic Inc., 730 Broadway, New York, NY 10003.

No part of this publication may be reproduced in whole or in part, or stored in a retrieval system, or transmitted in any form or by any means, electronic, mechanical, photocopying, recording, or otherwise, without written permission of the publisher. For information regarding permission, write to Scholastic Inc., 730 Broadway, New York, NY 10003.

ISBN 0-590-41450-X

Copyright © 1987 The Walt Disney Company. All rights reserved. Published by Scholastic Inc.

12 11 10 9 8 7 6 5 4 3   9/8 0 1 2/9

Printed in the U.S.A.   11

First Scholastic printing, December 1987

1

The story of Lady and the Tramp begins one Christmas day, a long while ago. In those days, women still wore dresses to their ankles. Horses still pulled buggies down rough cobblestone streets.

As you know, many things have changed since then. But some things, some very important things, remain the same. In those days, just as now, people put up Christmas trees to celebrate the holiday season. People also exchanged presents with those they loved. Unfortunately, too, just as today, some people were privileged, and some people were poor. There has always been, and there may always be, a right side of town . . . and a wrong side of town.

This particular Christmas, snow fell softly on the quaint little village where Jim Dear and Darling lived. They were young, newly married, and very much in love. Jim had chosen a very special present for Darling.

"Will she like it?" he wondered. "It *is* a little unusual."

Jim went to the tree and picked up the present. He had wrapped it in a hatbox.

"For you, Darling," he said. "Merry Christmas."

Darling took the box.

"Oh, Jim Dear," she said. "It's the hat I was admiring, isn't it? The one trimmed with ribbons."

A small pair of eyes peeped out from under the lid.

"Well," Jim smiled. "It does have a ribbon."

Darling reached into the box and felt something soft and furry. She lifted it out. It was a puppy, a sweet little cocker spaniel. Darling held the puppy to her cheek. It gave her a warm, friendly lick.

"Do you like her, Darling?" asked Jim.

"Oh, I love her," said Darling. "What a perfectly beautiful little lady."

2

And so, Lady got her name. She also got a special place to sleep. About this, Jim had a very set idea. When it was time for bed, he prepared a wicker basket with a soft cushion and set it in a corner of the kitchen.

"Come on, Lady," he called. "Over here."

Lady scampered across the floor and into his arms. Jim picked her up and placed her in the basket.

"There now, a nice little bed for you," he said.

"But Jim Dear," asked Darling, "are you sure she'll be warm enough?"

Jim turned down the gaslight.

"Of course, Darling," he said. "She'll go right to sleep."

When Jim Dear and Darling started out of the kitchen, Lady pushed at the door and followed, right behind them.

"Look," said Darling. "She's lonesome. Don't you think maybe, just for tonight. . . ?"

"Now, Darling," said Jim, "if we're going to show her who's master, we must be firm from the very beginning."

Jim put Lady back in bed and blocked the kitchen door with a chair. Lady tried to follow, but this time, she could not push the door open. She started to cry and then to howl. Loudly.

"Lady!" Jim called from the upstairs bedroom. "Stop that!"

Lady whimpered some more.

"Quiet now!" called Jim. "Back to bed!"

Lady pushed harder against the door. First she pushed through her nose, then her head, then her whole body. She was out! She stood at the bottom of the stairs and looked up. The stairway was tall and steep. Lady was very small, and her legs were short, but she pulled herself up the long steps, one by one.

Lady padded into the bedroom and up to the bed. Jim was now fast asleep. Lady pawed at the covers.

"Uh, what, what?" said Jim, sleepily. He picked Lady up and laid her at the foot of the bed.

"Aw, Jim," smiled Darling, happy.

Lady licked Darling's hand and settled down to sleep.

"But remember," said Jim, "just for tonight!"

3

Many months later, Lady was, of course, still sleeping on the bed. By this time she had grown from a puppy into a beautiful young dog.

This fine, sunshiney morning, it was still very early. Outside, a cock crowed. Lady stirred. She stretched, jumped off the bed, and tugged at Jim's foot.

"All right, Lady," he said. "I'm up. I'm up." He looked at the clock. "Oh, no," he said, as he remembered. "Doesn't Lady understand about Sundays?"

Lady bounded down the steps and out the small, dog-sized swinging door that led to the backyard. There were many things to do that morning. There were birds to bark at. There were bones to bury. Lady chased around the yard, busy at one thing and another. She stopped. She spied something. It was a pair of beady eyes, glinting at her from under the woodpile.

A rat! Lady barked. The rat ran to the edge of

the pile and stood up on its hind legs. Lady chased it as it ran through the woodpile and across the yard. Lady was quick, but the rat was quicker. It scrambled under a hole in the fence and disappeared across the alley.

Lady scratched at the fence. She would have tried to chase the rat, but right then the paperboy rode by. He rang the bell of his bicycle and tossed the morning paper into Lady's yard. Lady jumped to catch it. She ran back up the stairs and through the swinging door. She tore the paper as she squeezed through.

That morning, at breakfast, Jim read the torn paper as best he could.

"Have you noticed, Darling?" he asked. "Since we've had Lady, we see less and less of those disturbing headlines."

Jim poured some of his coffee into a saucer and set it down for Lady to drink.

"I don't know how we ever got along without her," Darling smiled. She handed Lady a doughnut.

"Say," said Jim. He'd suddenly remembered. "Lady must be about six months old now. We'd better be getting her a license."

4

The collar that Darling bought Lady was blue and very pretty. Lady's new license dangled from it just so.

"My, but it does look nice," said Darling. She adjusted the collar on Lady's neck. "So grown up. Won't Jock and Trusty be surprised?"

Lady looked at herself in the mirror, then scampered out the door. She couldn't wait to show her friends. Jock was in his yard, burying a bone.

"Oh, Jock!" called Lady.

"Oh, it's you, lassie," he said. Jock was a little black scottie and spoke with a Scottish lilt.

"Notice anything different?" Lady asked. She jingled her collar in his face.

"Why, lassie," he said. "A bonnie new collar." He sniffed it. "Hmm," he said. "It must be very expensive."

The two dogs trotted off across the yard to show their other friend.

Trusty, an old bloodhound, was fast asleep on

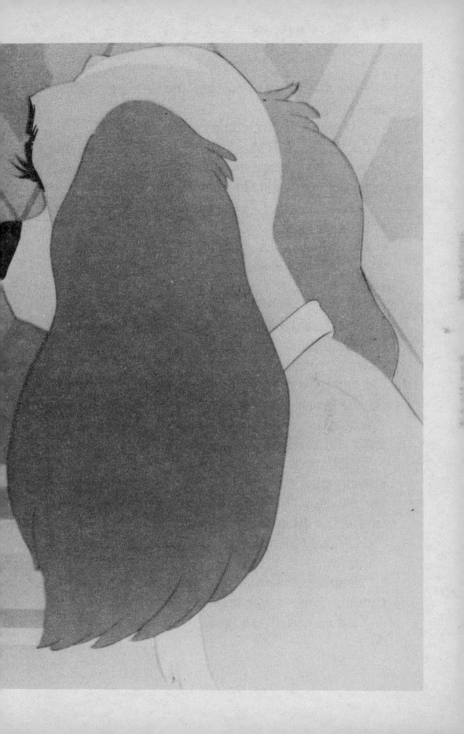

his porch. He was snorting and snoring, sniffing and twitching.

"He must be dreaming," said Lady.

"Aye," said Jock, "dreaming of those bonnie bygone days when he and his grandfather were tracking criminals through the swamps."

"Trusty did *that?*" asked Lady. Her eyes opened wide.

Just then, with a snort, Trusty awoke. Like Jock, he was pleased and proud to see Lady's new collar.

"My, my," he said. "How time does fly."

"Aye," said Jock. "It seems only yesterday she was cuttin' her teeth on Jim Dear's slippers, and now there she is — a full-grown lady."

Lady tossed her head proudly, jingling her tag. As Jock and Trusty said, she was wearing the greatest honor man could bestow, the badge of faith and responsibility.

Trusty was reminded of a story. "As my old grandpappy, Old Reliable, used to say," he began. He paused. "I don't recollect if I've ever mentioned Old Reliable before. . . ."

"Aye, you have, laddie," said Jock, with a sigh.

Just then, Jim Dear whistled for Lady.

"Please excuse me," she said, and she took off, running to meet her master at the walk.

"Ladies first," Jim said, when they got to the door.

14

Later that night, Jim Dear and Darling settled in front of the fireplace. Lady lay cozily at their feet.

"You know, Darling," said Jim, "with Lady here, I'd say life is quite complete."

"Yes, dear," said Darling. "I don't imagine anything could ever take her place in our hearts."

5

In another part of town, in a rougher neighborhood, there lived another dog. His name was Tramp. Tramp was a mutt and had no home.

Tramp often slept beside some train tracks, inside a water barrel. This morning when he woke up, he was thirsty, so he drank from a puddle. Then to wash himself, he stood under a dripping pipe.

"Brrr! What a day!" he said. He set off to find some breakfast.

Tramp was friends with many of the storekeepers in the neighborhood. People liked Tramp. They gave him food. Tramp decided he would have his breakfast at Tony's Restaurant. He trotted down the back alley and scratched at the kitchen door.

Joe, the man who worked in the kitchen, had saved a choice bone for Tramp. He tossed it out the door. Tramp trotted off happily, bone in mouth. He found a nice place behind a fence to sit and eat his breakfast.

On the other side of the fence, a wagon rolled up. It was the dogcatcher. He was posting notices. The notice said that any dog without a license would be caught and taken to the pound.

Tramp, of course, didn't have a license, and neither did any of his friends. In fact, the dogcatcher had already picked up a couple of strays. Tramp crept around the fence to peek in the back of the wagon. They *were* friends of his! It was Bull and Peg!

"Psst!" he whispered. "I'll try to get you out."

Tramp jumped up to the back of the wagon and opened the latch.

"Okay, get goin'," he said. "Scram!"

Bull and Peg escaped, but not before the dogcatcher saw them. He ran back to the wagon.

"Hey, what's going on over there?" he said.

Tramp bit his leg.

"Let go! Let go!" shouted the dogcatcher. "Why, you mangy mutt! I'll get you for this!"

Tramp took off running, and the dogcatcher took off after him. Tramp ran across the street and jumped over a wall. He hid behind a gate. The dogcatcher ran right by him. Tramp grinned.

When he was sure the coast was clear, Tramp stepped out. He took a look around.

"Well," he said. "Snob Hill." He was now in the rich part of town. "Huh," he smiled. "I wonder what the leash-and-collar set does for excitement."

6

Not far from there, Lady was curled up by her dish of food. Birds were fluttering around her dish, eating from it, but Lady didn't care. She was very sad. Jim Dear and Darling had been acting strangely lately. It seemed to Lady that they didn't love her anymore.

Just the other day when Jim Dear had come home from work, Lady ran to meet him. But instead of patting her on the head or playing with her, as he usually did, Jim Dear had been cross. He shouted, "Down, Lady! Down!" He seemed to be worried only about Darling. He kept asking Darling about her "condition."

Then one afternoon, when Lady was ready to go for her walk, Darling wouldn't even take her. Lady brought the leash and dropped it at Darling's feet, but she said, "No, Lady. No walk today." Darling was knitting something, some tiny booties. Lady had just wanted to play. She picked up a ball of yarn in her mouth, but Darling swatted

at her. It hadn't hurt, really, but Darling had never struck her before.

Lady sat in the yard, looking sadly at her dish. That is the way Jock and Trusty found her when they came for their morning visit. Lady told her friends the whole sad story. Jock and Trusty knew right away what the problem was.

"As my grandpappy, Old Reliable, used to say," said Trusty. He paused. "Er, I don't recollect if I've ever mentioned Old Reliable before," he said.

"Aye, ya have, laddie," said Jock. "Frequently." Jock turned to Lady. "Now, lassie," he said. "Dinna take it too seriously. After all, at a time like this. . . ."

"The birds and the bees," said Trusty. "The stork."

Lady looked at them, confused.

"What he's trying to say, lassie," said Jock, "is that Darling is expecting a wee bairn."

"Bairn?" asked Lady.

"He means a baby," said Trusty.

"Oh," said Lady, confused. "What's a baby?"

Jock and Trusty looked at each other. How in the world would they ever explain a baby?

"Well, they resemble humans, but I'd say a mite smaller," said Trusty.

"Aye, and they walk on all fours," said Jock.

"They beller a lot, but they're mighty sweet," said Trusty.

"And verra, verra soft," said Jock.

From behind a nearby gatepost, Tramp had listened to the whole conversation. He stood up and stepped into the yard. He was grinning.

"Babies are just a cute little bundle of trouble," he laughed.

Jock and Trusty looked at Tramp. Who was this new dog? He was just a mutt. Lady looked, too. She had never before seen a dog quite like Tramp.

7

Tramp trotted across the drive and over to the dogs.

"Yeah," he said. "Babies. They scratch, pinch, pull ears. . . ."

Tramp squeezed into the space between Jock and Lady and sat himself down.

"Looka here, laddie," said Jock angrily. "Who are you to barge in and — "

"The voice of experience, buster," said Tramp, with a smile.

Tramp had a lot to say about babies, and Lady listened to him, wide-eyed.

"Once a baby comes," he said, "the humans won't let you bark. They'll yell at you, say you're waking the baby."

Tramp told Lady that, with a baby in the house, she should never again expect juicy leftover scraps from dinner.

"They'll use them for baby food," he said.

Also, he told her, once the baby came, she

wouldn't even be allowed in the house. The humans would put her out in the cold, leaky doghouse, even in the worst weather.

"Dinna listen to him, lassie," said Jock. "No human is that cruel."

"Of course not, Miss Lady," said Trusty. "Why, everybody knows a dog's best friend is his human."

Tramp burst into laughter.

"Oh, come on now, fellas," he said. "You haven't fallen for that old line, have you?"

Jock had had enough of Tramp's unwanted advice.

"Aye!" he said, glaring at the dog. "And we've no need for mongrels and their radical ideas! Off with ye! Off with ye!"

"Okay, okay," said Tramp. He backed away toward the gate. But before he left, he turned to give Lady one last piece of advice.

"Remember this, Pigeon," he said. "A human heart has only so much room for love and affection. When a baby moves in, a dog moves out."

Lady watched, bewildered, as Tramp walked away and out the gate.

8

As the months passed, Jim Dear and Darling spent a lot of time preparing for the new baby. Jim Dear was hoping the baby would be a boy. He bought a baseball glove and a sports pennant to hang in the nursery. Darling was hoping for a girl. She spent long hours writing out lists of girls' names and choosing her favorites.

"Darling," said Jim one day. "There isn't any way we can tell for sure what it's going to be, is there?" he asked.

"I'm afraid not," said Darling. "No one ever knows for certain."

Autumn passed into winter. Darling began to have odd cravings for strange foods — watermelon and chop suey. She'd send Jim out in the snow for them, in the middle of the night. Winter passed into spring. Friends came to visit, bringing baby presents — little booties, little bonnets. The baby was due in April. It seemed that it would never come.

One day, though, one rainy April day, the baby did arrive. Lady had noticed the doctor's buggy parked outside the house. Jim came running down the stairs and went to the phone.

"Aunt Sarah!" he yelled into the receiver. "It's a boy! A boy!"

Aunt Sarah tried to ask Jim about the baby, but Jim dropped the phone.

"His eyes!" he shouted. "What color are the baby's eyes? I forgot to look!"

Jim went running back upstairs to see his son. He left the phone receiver dangling. He left Aunt Sarah hanging on the other end.

"Hello!" came her voice. "Are you there? Jim! Hello?"

Lady sat in the kitchen, watching the scene. Jim was acting awfully strange. This baby business certainly seemed a mystery.

9

The household bustled with the care of the new baby. Diapers hung outside on the clothesline. Baby bottles lined the windowsill. But still Lady did not even know what a baby was. She had not yet gotten into the nursery.

Lady watched Jim come down the stairs from the baby's room. He was whistling happily. Lady decided to investigate. She ran past Jim and through the open bedroom door. Darling was there, carrying something very small. She placed it gently in the cradle and sang a lullabye to it softly.

"La La Lu, La La Lu,
Oh, my little star sweeper,
I'll sweep the stardust for you.
La La Lu, La La Lu,
Little soft, fluffy sleeper,
Here comes a pink cloud for you.
La La Lu, La La Lu,
Little wandering angel,

Fold up your wings, close your eyes.
La La Lu, La La Lu,
And may love be your keeper,
La La Lu, La La Lu."

Lady padded softly to the cradle and tried to peek in. She stood up, resting her paws on the wood, but the sides were too high for her to see. Jim came up behind Lady and lifted her up for a good look. Darling pulled back the blanket so Lady could see. There, in the cradle, was the new baby. Lady wagged her tail happily.

"There now, little star sweeper," said Darling. She tucked the blanket back around her son. "Dream on," she said.

Lady liked this new baby. She didn't mind at all if he stayed. As time passed, she grew fonder and fonder of him. And also, she became very protective. One morning, when the baby had already been in the house for some time, Lady saw Jim and Darling packing their suitcases. They were slipping quietly down the stairs.

"Darling!" called Jim. "Come on! We haven't much time."

"Oh, Jim," said Darling. "I just can't leave him. He's still so small and helpless."

"He'll be all right," said Jim. "Come on. If he wakes up, we'll never get away."

Lady didn't know what to think. She ran down

the stairs and stood in front of Jim and Darling. She blocked their way. She growled.

"Hey, what's the matter with Lady?" asked Jim.

"Oh," said Darling. "She thinks we're running out on the baby."

Darling patted Lady on the head and explained. Of course they weren't running out on the baby, she said. They'd be back in a few days. They were leaving the baby with Lady, and also with Aunt Sarah, who would take care of him. The doorbell rang. Aunt Sarah had arrived.

Jim and Darling took their leave. Aunt Sarah carried her things into the house.

"Good-bye!" she called after Jim and Darling. Lady sat in the doorway, looking after them. When Aunt Sarah had waved a last good-bye, she let the door slam. Lady was locked outside.

"Now," said Aunt Sarah, "to see that nephew of mine."

She headed up the stairs.

10

Lady ran around to the back of the house to her swinging door. She jumped through and ran up the stairs. Aunt Sarah was already in the baby's room, leaning over the crib.

"Coochie-coochie," she was saying. "Coochie-coochie."

When Aunt Sarah saw Lady, she shooed her out of the room.

"What are you doing here?" she said crossly. "Go on now. Shoo! Scat!" She slammed the door in Lady's face. Lady walked dejectedly downstairs.

In the front hall stood a basket that Aunt Sarah had brought with her. Out from under the lid leered two pairs of eyes. As Lady watched, two cats jumped out. They were Siamese cats, and they began to sing:

"We are Siamese, if you please,
We are Siamese, if you don't please.

Now we are looking over our new domicile
   awhile.
If we like, we stay for maybe quite a while."

The two cats wasted no time making themselves
at home . . . and making trouble. They walked
haughtily into the parlor and crept up to the bird
cage. One cat leaped up and clawed at the bird.
Lady ran in barking, just in time.

Lady chased the cats away from the cage and
across the room. One cat knocked over a vase of
flowers. The other scratched the wood of the piano.
Both ran toward the goldfish bowl.

The goldfish bowl was set on top of a runner on
a table. The cats tugged at the runner, pulling the
bowl to the edge. As they did, they sang:

"Do you see that thing swimming 'round
   and 'round?
Maybe we could reaching in and make it
   drown
If we sneaking up upon it carefully
There will be a head for you, a tail for me."

The bowl crashed to the floor. Lady grabbed
the fish up to save it from the cats and dropped
it back in the bowl.

The cats, however, already had a new plan.
They heard the baby crying and crept up the stairs.
Again, they sang:

"Do you hear what I hear?
Purr . . . A baby crying!
Where we finding baby, there are milk
    nearby.
If we look in baby buggy,
There could be
Plenty milk for you and also some for me."

When Lady realized what the cats were up to, she chased them away from the nursery, back downstairs, and into the parlor. The cats leaped up to the curtains. The curtains came crashing down on Lady. Aunt Sarah heard the crash.

"What's going on down there?" she called.

When she got to the parlor, she gasped at the mess. Aunt Sarah didn't suspect her cats of the mischief.

"My darlings!" she said to them. "My precious pets."

She glared at Lady.

"Oh, that wicked animal," she said.

She grabbed Lady and took her to the nearest pet store.

"Good afternoon, ma'am," said the salesclerk. "What can I do for you?"

Aunt Sarah set Lady on the counter.

"I want a muzzle," she said. "A good, strong muzzle."

11

The salesclerk pulled a muzzle and leash out from behind the counter.

"Here's our latest muzzle," he said. "We'll just slip it on like this."

The clerk fastened the muzzle over Lady's head. What was this man doing? Why was he clamping her mouth shut? Lady struggled wildly, trying to get free.

"Lady, quiet!" said Aunt Sarah.

"Nice doggie. Don't wiggle," said the clerk.

Lady jumped to the floor, knocking Aunt Sarah to the ground. Then she dashed out the door.

"Come back!" called Aunt Sarah. "Come back here, I say!"

Lady ran, frightened, into the busy street outside. Car wheels sped by. Bicycles, trucks.

Lady ran up an alley. The other dogs in the neighborhood saw her and chased after her. Lady was no match for street dogs. They chased her up the alley and across some railroad tracks.

As it happened, Tramp was near the tracks. When he saw Lady, he took off after the pack. The pack of dogs chased Lady down a deserted alley. It was a dead end. They had her cornered against a wall. Lady crouched in fear.

Just as the dogs were about to pounce, Tramp jumped over the wall. He stood between the dogs and Lady and bared his teeth, snarling.

As Lady cowered behind a crate, a fierce fight broke out. It was Tramp alone against all the others. It looked as if the pack of dogs might win, but Tramp was determined to protect Lady. He lunged first at one dog, then another. The dogs ran away scared, their tails between their legs. Tramp chased every last one of them away.

"Hey, Pidge," Tramp called, when it was all over. Lady came cautiously out from behind the crate. "What are you doing on this side of the tracks?" Tramp asked.

Then he saw her muzzle.

"Aw, you poor kid," he said. "We gotta get this off."

Tramp picked up her leash in his mouth and led her away.

"Come on!" he said. "I think I know the very place."

12

Tramp led Lady to the zoo.

"The zoo?" asked Lady.

When they got there, a policeman was patrolling the entrance.

"We can't go in," said Lady.

"Why not?" asked Tramp.

"The sign says 'No Dogs Allowed,' " said Lady.

Tramp had an idea. He waited. A man walked through the entrance, into the zoo. Tramp followed him, easy as you please. The policeman stopped them.

"What's the matter? Can't you read?" he shouted at the man.

The man looked down at Tramp beside him.

"Oh. Why, he's not my dog," the man said. Tramp jumped up and licked the man in the face.

"Go away!" said the man. "Go away!" The man dropped his book. Tramp picked it right up.

"Not your dog, eh?" asked the policeman. "So I'm a liar, am I?"

The policeman grabbed the man by the collar. Tramp ran around and bit the policeman on his rear end.

"Ooh!" cried the policeman. "Pull a knife on me, will ya?"

A fight broke out between the men.

"Come on, Pidge," Tramp called.

Lady ran through the gate, and the two disappeared into the zoo.

Tramp and Lady walked past the ape cage and past the hyena.

"Timber!" someone suddenly shouted. A tree crashed down around them.

"What harebrained idiot is chopping down trees?" Tramp shouted. He looked up. It was a beaver. A beaver! If the beaver could bite through trees, he could bite through. . . .

"There's the answer to our problem," exclaimed Tramp. "Pardon me, friend," he shouted over. "I wonder if you'd do us a little favor?"

The beaver, true to reputation, was very busy. "Don't have a minute," he said as he worked. "Gots to cut the trees first, and then I gots to haul 'em. 'Tain't the cuttin' takes the time. It's the doggone haulin'."

"The hauling," said Tramp, thinking quickly. "Exactly! What you need is a log puller."

The beaver stopped short. "Log puller?" he asked. He was suddenly very interested.

"By lucky coincidence," said Tramp, "you see before you, modeled by the lovely little lady, the new, improved, patented, handy-dandy, never-fail, little, giant log puller! It cuts hauling time . . . *sixty-six percent!*"

That was all a busy beaver needed to hear. He wanted to put the thing on right away and try it out. He pulled at Lady's leash.

"How do you get this consarned thing off?" he asked.

"Glad you brought that up," said Tramp. "Simply place this strap between your teeth and bite. Hard."

"Like this?" asked the beaver.

The beaver bit. The muzzle fell off. Lady moved her mouth stiffly. She was free at last.

Lady and Tramp turned to go.

"It's all yours," Tramp said to the beaver, smiling.

"A free sample," said Lady.

"Thanks a lot," said the beaver. He slipped the muzzle over his own head and went right back to work.

13

Now that Lady was free of the muzzle, Tramp had plans for the evening, big plans. It wasn't every day that he found Lady on this side of the tracks. Tramp thought he'd show her the sights.

Tramp sniffed the evening air. In houses all around, people were cooking dinner.

"Something tells me it's suppertime," he said.

Since this was such a special night, Tramp took Lady to Tony's. He brought her up the back alley and scratched at the kitchen door. Tony came to answer. Tony was very glad to see Tramp.

"Where have you been so long?" he asked. "Hey, Joe, look who's here."

Lady peeked her head timidly out from behind some boxes.

"He's got a new girl friend!" said Tony.

"Well, son'a'ma gun," said Joe.

Tony brought a table out from the restaurant and set it up in the alley. He brought a candle out, so the couple could eat by candlelight. Joe went inside and dished up a big plate of spaghetti and meatballs. No mere bones for Tramp tonight. Tramp and Lady would get the best in the house.

As the dogs ate, Tony and Joe serenaded them. They sang an old Italian song, one about love.

"For this is the night, it's a beautiful night,
And we call it Bella Notte.
Look at the skies,
They have stars in their eyes,
On this lovely Bella Notte.
Side by side with your loved one
You'll find enchantment here.
The night will weave its magic spell
When the one you love is near.
For this is the night, it's a beautiful night,
And we call it Bella Notte."

Lady and Tramp ate their dinner under the stars and listened to the music. As they slurped up the strands of spaghetti, their mouths met in the middle. It was their first, shy kiss.

After dinner, Tramp and Lady took a walk. They sat by a quiet lake lit by a silver moon. Tramp and Lady were surprised and taken by what was happening to them. Lady and the Tramp found themselves falling in love.

14

When morning dawned, Lady and the Tramp were sleeping soundly on the side of a hill. A cock crowed. Lady opened her eyes.

"Oh, dear," she said. "I should've been home hours ago."

Tramp wanted Lady to stay with him.

"There's a great big hunk of world out there," he said, "with no fence around it. It's ours for the taking."

Lady considered. Two dogs on the loose. It did sound like fun, but she had other worries.

"Who'd watch over the baby?" she asked.

Tramp shrugged. That was his answer. "Come on," he said. "I'll take you home."

On the way to Lady's house, the two dogs passed a chicken coop.

"Ever chase chickens?" asked Tramp.

"I should say not," said Lady.

"Ho ho! Then you've never lived," said Tramp. "Come on."

Tramp dug his way under the fence and into the yard. Lady followed. The chickens were still asleep but not for long. Tramp ran barking through the coop, and the chickens woke up, all a-flutter. They squawked wildly. Their feathers flew.

"Fun, eh?" Tramp asked Lady.

"Hey!" called a man's voice suddenly. "What's going on in there?"

The man ran into the coop. He had a gun, and he shot at the dogs.

Tramp and Lady tore off, back under the fence and away from the yard.

"Whee!" yelled Tramp, as they ran, "this is living!"

At last the two were out of gunshot. Tramp kept running, and Lady followed, but she was slower. Before Lady knew what was happening to her, a net swooped down and caught her. It was the dogcatcher! He locked her in his wagon and drove off with her.

Tramp stopped running to rest. He looked around. Where was Lady?

"Pidge!" he called. "Pigeon! Where are you?"

Tramp ran back the way they had come, calling for Lady. What could have happened to her? She had been right behind him. Tramp was struck with fear.

15

At the pound, there were many dogs. All were mutts and strays. Bull was there. Peg was there. These were dogs who had seen their share of trouble. None was purebred like Lady.

The dogcatcher brought Lady in. He pulled her by a rough rope and locked her in one of the cages. The male dogs gathered around. The dogcatcher left Lady to the hounds.

"Well, well. Look, you'se guys," said one. "Miss Park Avenue herself."

"Blimey," said Bull. "A regular debutante."

One tough dog walked up close to Lady and eyed her license.

"Hey," he said. "Take a look at the crown jewel she's wearing."

All the dogs laughed.

Peg, who lay in a corner of the cage, heard the laughter. When she saw what was going on, she pushed her way through the crowd.

"All right, you guys. Lay off," she said. "Can't

you see the poor kid's scared enough?"

"Pay no attention to them," piped in another dog. "Wearing a license in front of them is like waving a red flag in front of a bull."

"My license?" asked Lady. "What's the matter with it?"

Of course, there was nothing the matter with Lady's license. The problem was, she had one and the other dogs didn't.

"Honey, they're jealous," said Peg. "That's your passport to freedom."

Peg was interrupted by a noise down the hall. A guard had opened a cage and taken out one dog. He led the dog down the hall. The other dogs watched, suddenly silent.

"Where is he taking him?" asked Lady.

"On the long walk, sister," said the tough dog. "Through the one-way door."

Lady opened her eyes in fright. "You mean . . . you mean . . . he's. . . ."

The other dog nodded solemnly.

"Oh, well," said Bull. "A short life and a merry one."

"Yeah," said his friend. "That's what the Tramp always says."

"The Tramp?" asked Lady. She looked up in surprise.

16

All the dogs knew the Tramp. He was a dog with a reputation.

"That's a bloke that never gets caught," said Bull.

Peg turned to Lady. "You won't believe this, dearie," she said, "but no matter how tight a jam he's in, that Tramp always finds a way out."

All the dogs agreed; Tramp was king. But they also knew his weakness.

"Dames," said the tough one.

"He does have an eye for a well-turned paw," said Bull.

Apparently, Tramp had many girl friends.

"There's Lulu," said Bull, "Trixie and Fifi. . . ."

"And my sister, Rosita Chiquita Juanita," said a little Chihuahua.

"What a dog!" said Peg, with a sigh. Peg was obviously taken by the Tramp herself.

Peg, a chorus dog by trade, leaned against the bars and sang:

"He's a tramp, but they love him.
Breaks a new heart every day.
He's a tramp, they adore him,
And I only hope he'll stay that way.
He's a tramp, he's a scoundrel.
He's a rounder, he's a cad.
He's a tramp, but I love him.
Yes, even I have got it pretty bad.
You can never tell when he'll show up.
He gives you plenty of trouble.
I guess he's just a no-count pup,
But I wish that he were double.
He's a tramp, he's a rover,
And there's nothing more to say.
If he's a tramp, he's a good one,
And I wish that I could travel his way.
Wish that I could travel his way."

Lady was learning quite a bit about her friend
the Tramp. When Peg finished her song, the dogs
spoke up. Tramp was free and wild right now,
they agreed, but someday that had to change.
Someday he was going to meet a girl who'd make
him want to settle down.

"Someone like Miss Park Avenue here?" asked
Bull.

"Could be," one answered. He frowned. "But
when that happens," he said, "Tramp'll grow care-

less. And that's when the dogcatcher will finally catch him."

"That'll be curtains for the Tramp," said the tough dog.

Lady looked at him in fright.

Just then the guard came back to let Lady out. He had checked her license number, and she could go free.

"They've come to take you home," he said to Lady. "You're too nice a girl to be in this place."

17

When Lady got home, Aunt Sarah put her out back in the doghouse and chained her to a stake. Jock and Trusty trotted over to cheer poor Lady up. They were thinking maybe one of them ought to propose to Lady. If Lady were to marry one or the other, she could start a new life. Then she could forget the whole, horrible ordeal she'd just been through.

Before they could actually get the proposal out, another dog wandered into the yard. It was Tramp! Trusty and Jock glared at him. Lady turned her back.

"Looks like I'm the one that's in the doghouse," said Tramp.

"You mongrel!" shouted Jock.

"We'll gladly throw the rascal out!" said Trusty.

"That won't be necessary, thank you," Lady said to her friends. "I can take care of the matter myself."

Jock and Trusty growled at Tramp, then turned

haughtily home. Lady looked Tramp in the eye.

"It wasn't my fault, Pigeon," Tramp said quickly. "I thought you were right behind me. Honest! And when I heard they'd taken you to the pound — "

"Don't even mention that horrible place," cried Lady. "I was so embarrassed. And frightened."

"Aw," said Tramp. "Now who could ever harm a cute little trick like you?"

"Trick?" Lady said angrily. "Trick? That reminds me. Who is Trixie? And Lulu? And Fifi? And Rosita Chiquita?"

Tramp knew he was in trouble. He tried to sidle up to Lady, but she stuck her nose in the air. She walked away, as far as her chain would allow.

"I don't care if the dogcatcher *does* catch you!" she shouted. "Good-bye!"

Lady disappeared into her doghouse, crying. Tramp walked dejectedly away. He let himself out through the hole in the fence.

Tramp was gone, but another animal, one much smaller and much sneakier, scurried across the alley. It slipped through the fence and into Lady's yard.

18

The rat! He ran across the woodpile and past Lady. Lady jumped up and barked. She charged. She almost caught the rat by the tail, but was stopped short by her chain.

The rat scampered to the trellis that went up the side of the house. He started to climb. Lady barked furiously. Aunt Sarah appeared in the window, disturbed by the barking.

"Stop that!" she called down.

The rat climbed up the trellis and across the roof. He ran to the nursery window and started to climb through. Lady pulled at her chain, barking as loudly as she could.

"Stop that racket!" Aunt Sarah shouted.

Luckily, Tramp had also heard Lady's barking. He ran into the yard.

"What's wrong, Pidge?" he asked.

"A rat! In the baby's room!" said Lady.

Tramp ran through the small swinging door and into the house. By the time he reached the nurs-

ery, the rat was already creeping toward the baby's crib. Tramp chased it. He pounced on the rat, but the rat bit and scratched him. The rat escaped.

Outside, Lady pulled at her chain, finally breaking free. She raced up the stairs. When she ran into the nursery, the rat was crawling up the corner of the crib. Tramp leaped at the rat. He knocked over the crib. Tramp chased the rat behind a chair. He killed it. Tramp and Lady saved the baby.

When Aunt Sarah heard all the commotion, she burst into the room. What she saw was a shambles. The crib was knocked over and so was a lamp. Aunt Sarah picked up the baby and shouted at the dogs.

"You vicious brutes!" she yelled. "Back! Get back!"

Aunt Sarah locked Tramp in a closet and then locked Lady in the cellar. She went right to the phone and called the pound. She told the dogcatcher she'd caught Tramp.

"I insist you pick him up immediately," she said.

19

When Jim Dear and Darling got home, they were surprised to see the pound wagon in their front drive. The dogcatcher was leading Tramp into the wagon. Aunt Sarah watched, victorious.

"If you want my advice," she said, "you'll destroy that animal at once."

"Don't worry," said the dogcatcher. "We've been after this one for months. We'll take care of him."

Jim hurried up to the wagon. "What's going on here?" he asked.

"Just picking up a stray, mister," said the dogcatcher. "Caught him attacking a baby."

Just then, Jock and Trusty walked up and overheard. So Tramp had attacked the baby, had he?

"I knew all along he was no good," said Jock.

Lady scratched at the cellar door. Jim opened it, and Lady raced up the stairs, into the nursery. She was barking insistently.

"She's trying to tell us something," said Jim.

He ran after her. "What is it, old girl?"

Lady ran up to the chair, barking.

"Ah!" shrieked Aunt Sarah. "A rat!"

Suddenly, Jock and Trusty understood.

"I misjudged Tramp," said Jock. "Badly."

"Come on!" said Trusty. "We've got to stop that wagon!"

Jock and Trusty raced out of the house and down the street. They didn't know exactly which way the wagon had gone, but they knew they had to find it.

"Follow the scent!" said Trusty. He put his nose to the ground and took off, hot on the trail.

There was the wagon! Jock and Trusty bounded after the galloping horses.

Jock ran alongside the wagon's wheels. Trusty ran in front of the horses. The horses reared up. The wagon tipped over. Tramp fell against the bars.

Jim, Darling, and Lady were also chasing the wagon. They had hopped into a taxi, and the taxi sped to the scene. Lady jumped out when she saw Tramp. She jumped at the bars, barking happily.

On the other side of the wagon, Jock howled mournfully. When the wagon had fallen, it had fallen on Trusty. Trusty now lay trapped beneath a wheel. Jock nudged him. Trusty didn't move.

20

All things pass, and so did this. The seasons changed. Once again, it was Christmas. When the holiday arrived, there was not just one baby in Lady's house, there were four more. Well, four *puppies*, that is. Lady and the Tramp had had a litter. Three of the puppies looked very much like Lady. The other puppy looked very much like Tramp. You can be sure that one baby and four puppies added up to quite an active household.

On Christmas morning Jim hurried about, trying to get the baby and the puppies together for a picture. The baby shook his rattle in the puppies' faces. The puppies pulled at the baby's pajamas. No one would sit still. Jim glanced out the window.

"Visitors," he announced.

Up the walk came Jock . . . and Trusty! Trusty was alive! His foot was bandaged with a splint.

"Careful now, mon," said Jock, helping his friend. "It's a wee bit slippery."

Jim let the two dogs in and invited them into

the parlor. Jock and Trusty inspected the new pups. Lady and the Tramp looked on proudly.

"And I see you finally acquired a collar," Jock said to Tramp. Tramp looked a little embarrassed. He scratched himself.

"Yes," he said. "Complete with license."

"A new collar," said Trusty. "I caught the scent the moment I came in the house. Of course," he added, "my sense of smell is highly developed."

Jock smiled knowingly at Lady and Tramp.

"Runs in the family, you know," Trusty continued. The puppies gathered around him. "As my grandpappy, Old Reliable, used to say. . . ." He stopped. "Er, I don't recollect if I've ever mentioned Old Reliable before. . . ."

"No, you haven't, Uncle Trusty," said the pups.

"I haven't?" said Trusty. "Well, as Old Reliable used to say. . . . He'd say. . . . He'd say. . . ." Trusty shook his head, stumped.

"Doggone," he said. "You know, I clean forgot what it was he used to say!"

Everybody laughed. Trusty, too.

Outside, snow fell on the quiet village. Inside, the Christmas lights shone.